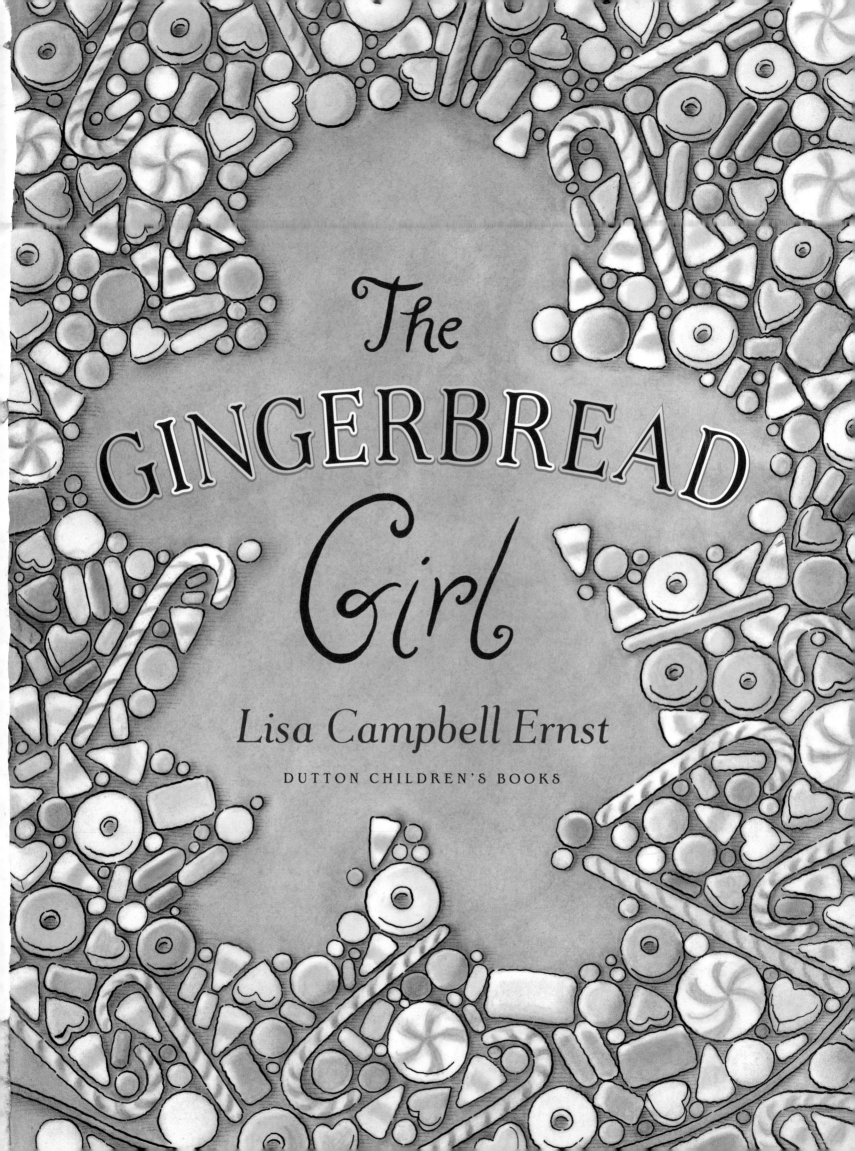

The GINGERBREAD Girl

Lisa Campbell Ernst

DUTTON CHILDREN'S BOOKS

DUTTON CHILDREN'S BOOKS
A division of Penguin Young Readers Group

PUBLISHED BY THE PENGUIN GROUP ❖ Penguin Group (USA) Inc., 375 Hudson Street, New York, New York 10014, U.S.A. ❖ Penguin Group (Canada), 90 Eglinton Avenue East, Suite 700, Toronto, Ontario, Canada M4P 2Y3 (a division of Pearson Penguin Canada Inc.) ❖ Penguin Books Ltd, 80 Strand, London WC2R 0RL, England ❖ Penguin Ireland, 25 St Stephen's Green, Dublin 2, Ireland (a division of Penguin Books Ltd) ❖ Penguin Group (Australia), 250 Camberwell Road, Camberwell, Victoria 3124, Australia (a division of Pearson Australia Group Pty Ltd) ❖ Penguin Books India Pvt Ltd, 11 Community Centre, Panchsheel Park, New Delhi - 110 017, India ❖ Penguin Group (NZ), Cnr Airborne and Rosedale Roads, Albany, Auckland 1310, New Zealand (a division of Pearson New Zealand Ltd) ❖ Penguin Books (South Africa) (Pty) Ltd, 24 Sturdee Avenue, Rosebank, Johannesburg 2196, South Africa ❖ Penguin Books Ltd, Registered Offices: 80 Strand, London WC2R 0RL, England

Library of Congress Cataloging-in-Publication Data
Ernst, Lisa Campbell.
The Gingerbread Girl / by Lisa Campbell Ernst. — 1st ed.
p. cm.
Summary: Like her older brother, the Gingerbread Boy, who was eventually devoured by a fox,
the Gingerbread Girl eludes the many people who would like to eat her but also has a plan to escape her sibling's fate.
ISBN 0-525-47667-9 (alk. paper) [1. Gingerbread—Fiction. 2. Foxes—Fiction. 3. Humorous stories.] I. Title.
PZ7.E7323Ghi 2006 [E]—dc22 2006004193

Published in the United States by Dutton Children's Books, a division of Penguin Young Readers Group
345 Hudson Street, New York, New York 10014 ❖ www.penguin.com/youngreaders
Designed by Heather Wood with Lisa Campbell Ernst
Manufactured in China ❖ First Edition
5 7 9 10 8 6 4

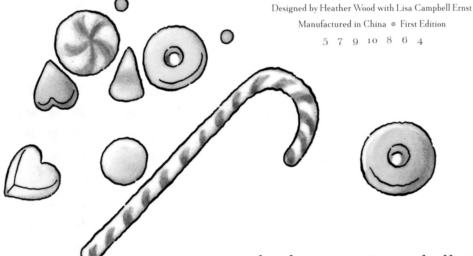

Also by Lisa Campbell Ernst

SYLVIA JEAN, DRAMA QUEEN

THE TURN-AROUND, UPSIDE-DOWN ALPHABET BOOK

TANGRAM MAGICIAN

THE LETTERS ARE LOST!

GOLDILOCKS RETURNS

LITTLE RED RIDING HOOD

SAM JOHNSON AND THE BLUE RIBBON QUILT

WAKE UP, IT'S SPRING!

To Keith and Becky,
who forged the way—
*with love and respect
from your baby sister*

You may remember the sad story
of the Gingerbread Boy.

He ran away from the lonely old
woman who baked him, as well as
many other hungry characters.

His dash through life
was ended in one greedy
gulp by a sly fox
pretending to help him
cross a river.

*This is the story of
his younger, wiser sister.*

A FULL YEAR HAD PASSED since the lonely old woman
and the lonely old man had lost their Gingerbread Boy to
the devious fox. They were even lonelier than before.

"Let's bake again," suggested the old man one morning.

"But what if the same thing happens?" cried the old
woman. "I couldn't bear the loss."

"Let's make a *girl* this time, and decorate her with
candies—surely a sweet little girl wouldn't run away!"
answered the man.

So they mixed up the dough, rolled it, and cut it out.
They dressed it with as many candies as they could fit,
completing the cookie with an amazing hairdo made
of licorice whips.

"She *is* sweet!" gasped the woman as she slid the
cookie sheet into the oven.

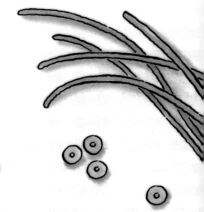

While the lonely old woman and the lonely old man stood watch by the oven, they talked, remembering their Gingerbread Boy's short life.

"He never should have run away."

"He never should have trusted that fox."

As the new cookie baked, her mind woke up, and she heard everything.

Sweet or not, she thought, *things will be different this time.*

When it was time for the cookie to be done, the old woman carefully—ever so carefully—cracked open the oven door to peek. . . .

BAM!

Out jumped the gingerbread cookie, running toward the door.

The little old woman screamed, "Stop! Stop!" and the little old man came running. But the cookie was already out the door and headed down the same path that her brother had traveled.

"Here we go," whispered the Gingerbread Girl.

The man and the woman chased after her, but she sang,

"I'll run and I'll run
With a leap and a twirl.
You can't catch me,
I'm the Gingerbread GIRL!"

As the Gingerbread Girl dashed along the path, she came to a group of farmers working in the fields. The aroma of fresh-baked gingerbread caught their attention.

"Wait!" the hungry farmers shouted, and began to run after the Gingerbread Girl. She laughed and called,

"Hey, farmers, don't bother!
Like my brother, I'm fast!
Run all you want,
But I've learned from his past!

"I'll run and I'll run
With a leap and a twirl.
You can't catch me,

I'm the Gingerbread GIRL!"

Farther down the road, a pig came into view. As the
Gingerbread Girl grew closer, her candy sparkled in
the sunlight. The pig squealed with joy and tried to
take a bite, but the Gingerbread Girl was too fast. She
leaped over him, singing,

"*I can leap past piggy*
Like all of the others.
This story will not end
Like that of my brother's!

"*I'll run and I'll run*
With a leap and a twirl.
You can't catch me,
I'm the Gingerbread GIRL!"

On down the path, she came upon an artist. "A masterpiece good enough to eat!" the artist whispered, and reached out to scoop up the Gingerbread Girl. With some fancy footwork the Gingerbread Girl zipped past, laughing.

"I can outrun this artist
Like I outran the pig.
I am one smart cookie
(despite this wild wig!).

"I'll run and I'll run
With a leap and a twirl.
You can't catch me,
I'm the Gingerbread GIRL!"

Farther along, the Gingerbread Girl passed a cow with her calf, who mooed happily, "Mama, I want a cookie to go with my milk!"

But when the cow tried to catch the Gingerbread Girl, she soon found herself running behind, listening to the Gingerbread Girl call,

"Chase if you want,
I am faster than you—
Although you have four feet,
And I've only two!

"I'll run and I'll run
With a leap and a twirl.
You can't catch me,
I'm the Gingerbread GIRL!"

Up ahead, a dog walker was crossing the path with three dogs. The dogs barked happily, seeing a tasty treat headed their way.

But as the Gingerbread Girl sped past, the group was soon in line with the others, hearing,

"You're joining the chase?
The more the merrier!
But no one can stop me,
Not hound, not terrier!

I'll run and I'll run
With a leap and a twirl.
You can't catch me,
I'm the Gingerbread GIRL!"

Now the path ran right past a school. The children
were out for recess and feeling quite hungry. Shouts of
"Coooookieeeee!!!!!" were heard across the playground.
The Gingerbread Girl waved to them all as they joined
the chase with their teachers, and she sang,

"I know that it's snack time,
And you want a sweet.
Come follow along,
And you'll soon have a treat.

"I'll run and I'll run
With a leap and a twirl.
You can't catch me,
I'm the Gingerbread GIRL!"

Finally, the Gingerbread Girl came to the same river her brother had tried to cross. Who should be waiting for her but that same devious fox.

"Hello, my pretty," crooned the fox. "I was a friend of your brother's. It looks like trouble runs in the family! Do let me help you across the river—just jump onto my tail."

The Gingerbread Girl shivered, then sang in nearly a whisper,

"Do I have your promise
For a safe ride to shore?
You won't drop me or eat me?
That's all I implore."

The fox chuckled. "I promise, my sweet little tidbit." And the Gingerbread Girl gingerly climbed on the fox's tail.

The instant the Gingerbread Girl climbed on, the fox dove into the water, ready for a fabulous feast.

"Ooooh, the water is so deep, move to my back!" he insisted, thinking this cute cookie was even dumber than her brother. Anyone could tell by looking at her that she was an airhead. The Gingerbread Girl did what she was told. "That's a good little girl," the fox said with a snicker. "Oh my, the water is deeper, now move to my head!"

No sooner had he spoken those words than the Gingerbread Girl leaped to his head, pulling off a strand of her own leathery licorice hair. With the expertise of a ranch hand, she triple-looped it around the fox's snout and tied it off with a half-hitch knot. "You're right," she whispered in the fox's ear. "I *am* good."

The fox snarled and struggled and strained, thrashing about, but the Gingerbread Girl hung on, turning him back toward the crowd. Riding the fox like a bucking bronco, the Gingerbread Girl whizzed past, singing,

"He'll run and he'll run

The awestruck crowd followed, all the way back
to the lonely old woman and the lonely old man's house.
The Gingerbread Girl rode into the kitchen, secured
the fox, jumped onto the table, and

She measured and mixed
With a leap and a twirl,
Singing, "I'll bake you some more,
I'm the Gingerbread GIRL!"

The old woman and man quickly joined in to help,
having a hungry, happy houseful to feed. From that
moment on, of course, they were *never* lonely again.

And what of the fox? The Gingerbread Girl was eventually able to teach him some manners, using gingerbread crumbs for treats. Most days you could see them riding across the countryside and hear a small voice drifting in the breeze:

"We'll run and we'll run

With a leap and a twirl.

I outfoxed the fox,

I'm the

Gingerbread

Girl!"